The Brothers Grimm

Sleeping Beauty

and other fairy tales

Miles Kelly

First published in 2015 by Miles Kelly Publishing Ltd
Harding's Barn, Bardfield End Green, Thaxted, Essex, CM6 3PX, UK

2 4 6 8 10 9 7 5 3 1

Publishing Director Belinda Gallagher
Creative Director Jo Cowan
Editorial Director Rosie Neave
Designer Rob Hale
Production Manager Elizabeth Collins
Reprographics Stephan Davis, Jennifer Cozens, Thom Allaway

ISBN 978-1-78209-742-6

Printed in China

British Library Cataloguing-in-Publication Data
A catalogue record for this book is available from the British Library

ACKNOWLEDGEMENTS
The publishers would like to thank the following artists who have contributed to this book:

Front cover and all border illustrations: Louise Ellis (The Bright Agency)

Inside illustrations:
Sleeping Beauty Polona Kosec (Advocate-art)
The Crystal Ball Atyeh Zeighami (Advocate-art)
The Donkey Martina Peluso (Advocate-art)
Jorinda and Joringel Lucia Masciullo (Pickled Ink)

Made with paper from a sustainable forest

www.mileskelly.net
info@mileskelly.net

Contents

Sleeping Beauty

Long ago, a king and queen reigned in a country far away. They waited a long time to have a child, and when the queen finally gave birth to a little girl, everyone in the land rejoiced. The proud king held a feast to celebrate. He invited all his family and nobles and friends and neighbours. And the joyful queen said, "We should invite the fairies too, so that they will always be kind and good to our little daughter."

Now there were thirteen fairies in the kingdom, but the king and queen had only twelve golden dishes for them to eat out of. So the royal couple decided not to invite one of the fairies.

The big day came and the twelve fairies arrived, each with a long white wand in her hand. And after the feast was over they gathered round the baby's cradle and each gave her a gift: goodness, beauty, intelligence, and so on – all the best things in the world.

Just as eleven of the fairies had finished, a great noise was heard in the courtyard. Into the feasting hall strode the thirteenth fairy, with a broomstick in her hand. As she had not been invited to the feast she was very angry. She swept up to the cradle and cried out: "When the princess is fifteen she shall be injured by a spinning wheel spindle and fall down dead."

The queen collapsed into the king's arms in shock, while everyone gasped and wept and wrung their hands, and the evil fairy stormed out.

Everyone had quite forgotten the twelfth of the friendly fairies, who had not yet given her gift. Now she stepped forward. "I'm afraid I cannot undo the evil curse," she sighed, "but perhaps I can soften it a little…" And she made a magic wish: that the princess would not die when the spindle injured her, only fall asleep for a hundred years.

The next day, the king did what he could to save his dear child: he ordered that all the spinning wheels in the kingdom should be burnt. And so the little princess grew up without ever seeing one. She became good and clever and beautiful – and all the other wonderful things the eleven good fairies had wished for her. Everyone who knew her, loved her.

On the day of her fifteenth birthday, the princess was walking through the palace when she came across a little door she had never noticed before. She opened it and there was the entrance to a mysterious tower. At the top of the tower steps sat an old lady, busy at a strange wheel with some thread.

"Hello," said the princess, very curious. "What are you doing?"

"Spinning," said the old lady, and hummed a tune while *whrrr!* went the wheel.

"How prettily that little thing turns round!" said the princess, reaching out for the spindle. "Ouch!" she cried as her fingers touched it.

And while the wicked fairy (for it was she) and her spinning wheel vanished, the princess fell down in an enchanted sleep.

At that moment the king and queen on their thrones in the great hall fell asleep too, and so did all the courtiers. The dogs slept by their feet, and so did the horses in the stables, the pigeons on the tops of the turrets and the flies upon the walls. In the kitchen the butler fell asleep while taking a drink of beer and the cook fell asleep while turning a goose on a spit – even the fire on the hearth stopped blazing. In the courtyard and gardens the fountains froze, the flowers stilled, and the royal guards nodded and slept soundly.

Days, weeks and then months went past and a large hedge of thorns soon grew round the palace. Every year it became higher and thicker, till at last the palace was surrounded and hidden, so that not even the roof or the chimneys could be seen. But people often told stories of the beautiful sleeping Briar Rose (for so the king's daughter was called). And from time to time, princes would find the thicket and try to break through to reach the palace. No one ever could, however, for the thorns and bushes grabbed them as if they had hands and held them fast.

On the very day that one hundred years had passed, a prince was riding near the thicket. To his astonishment the bushes parted as he approached to let him clamber through easily, and the sharp thorns turned into beautiful flowers as he passed them.

He came to the palace and walked

through the still courtyard, the silent gardens and the motionless halls, marvelling at how everything and everyone had been frozen in time. Finally, he passed through a strange little door and came to the small tower room where Princess Briar Rose lay asleep on the floor. She looked so beautiful that the prince stooped down and gave her a kiss.

At that moment she opened her eyes and woke up. And how she smiled at the handsome prince before her! He helped her up and together they went out into the palace – in which everyone else was waking up too, quite astonished.

Over the coming days, an even more splendid feast was held than at Briar Rose's birth – a feast to celebrate her marriage to the prince. And everyone lived happily ever after.

The Crystal Ball

There was once an enchantress with three sons who loved each other dearly. However, the old enchantress did not trust them and thought they wanted to steal her power from her. So she changed the eldest into an eagle, and he had to fly away and live in the mountains. She changed the second into a whale, and he was forced to live in the sea. But the third son managed to run away before his wicked mother turned him into a beast too.

At first the third son didn't know what to do with himself without his beloved brothers. But then he decided to rescue a king's daughter who was bewitched and imprisoned in a castle called the Castle of the Golden Sun. Many young men had already died trying. Still, the youngest son was brave and made up his mind to do his best.

He travelled for a long time seeking the castle, but he could not find it. One day, he was going through a forest when he came across two arguing giants, one of them holding a hat. "We both want the hat," one giant explained. "We cannot decide who it rightfully belongs to!"

"How can you fall out so badly about a hat?" asked the youth.

"It is no ordinary hat," said the second giant. "It is a wishing-hat. Whoever wears it can wish himself wherever he wants to go and in an instant he will be there."

Then the young man said, "Give me the hat. I will walk a short distance off and shout 'Go!'. You two start running and whoever reaches me first will win the hat."

The giants thought this was a brilliant idea and they gave him the wishing-hat. So the young man walked away and put on the hat and thought of the Castle of the Golden Sun. Immediately he found himself standing on a high mountain in front of the castle gate. He entered and climbed to the top of the highest tower, where he found the king's daughter. But how shocked he was. She had a wrinkly, grey face, red eyes and lank, greasy hair.

"Are you the king's daughter whom everyone says is so beautiful?" he asked politely, trying to hide his surprise.

"Yes," she answered, "but this is not what I really look like. I have been bewitched so I appear ugly." She held up a mirror. In it the young man saw himself reflected next to the most beautiful young lady in the world. "This is what I really look like," she explained, with tears rolling down her cheeks.

"However can I break the spell and set you free?" he urged.

And the princess said, "Go down the mountain and you will see a wild bull standing by a stream. You must fight it. Many young men have died trying. If you can kill it, a fiery bird will spring out of it. Inside the bird's body is a strange egg. And inside the egg is a crystal ball which holds the magic of the enchanter who bewitched me.

"If you can catch the fiery bird and get the crystal ball, bring it here to the enchanter in the great hall. His power will be destroyed. But the bird will burn you if you touch it. And if the egg falls on the ground it will blaze into flame and burn everything nearby with it, including the crystal ball."

So the youth went down the mountain to the stream. There stood the bull, snorting and bellowing. The bull charged at the young man, but he grabbed its horns and swung onto its back. As it tried to throw him off, he drew his sword, plunged it into the animal, and it fell down dead.

Straight away
a fiery bird flew
out of it, but it soared
away into the sky. Just as
the young man thought all
hope was lost an eagle – the young man's
brother – suddenly swooped down from the
clouds and hunted the fiery bird out to sea.

When at last the bird was exhausted at
being chased, it let its egg fall. The egg landed

on a fisherman's hut on the shore, which immediately burst into flames.

The young man started to despair once more, but then a whale came swimming towards the shore – it was the young man's other brother. It made a huge wave which surged over the hut and put out the flames.

When all was safe the youth hurried to look for the egg in the ruins. Luckily, it had not been totally destroyed – only the shell had melted, and he was able to take out the crystal ball unharmed.

Carefully, he carried it back to the Castle of the Golden Sun. He strode into the great hall, where the enchanter sat poring over his book of black magic, and held the crystal ball before him.

Then the sorcerer gave a cry of despair and disappeared in a flash of green fire.

The young man's heart soared. He hurried to find the king's daughter and, when he entered her room, he found her sitting there as her true, beautiful self. Next, he used the magic of the crystal ball to turn his faithful brothers back to their human form. Then they all lived happily in the Castle of the Golden Sun with the magic crystal ball to protect them, so no enchantresses or enchanters ever bothered them again.

The Donkey

Once upon a time there lived a king and a queen who were rich and had everything they wanted – except a child. Finally their wish was granted and the queen had a baby. But it was a little donkey!

The queen was terribly upset, but the king said bravely: "God has sent him to us. He is my son and heir to my throne. I command that no one will treat him any differently to a usual prince."

So the little donkey was brought up just the same as any royal child. The king ordered all the mirrors in the palace to be removed, so the little donkey didn't realize that he was different. He grew up happily and had a lovely nature. He liked to play and help people and he loved music, especially the lute. He studied hard and by the time he was grown up he had learned to strum the instrument with his hooves just as beautifully as any master musician.

One sunny day, the grown-up donkey-prince was out for a walk by himself when he happened to peer into a well that was full of glassy water. He saw his own reflection for the first time – and he was shocked and horrified.

He didn't know how he could face his family and friends now that he knew what he was, and so he ran away from the palace.

He travelled far and wide, and at last

he came to a kingdom where he heard the king had a beautiful daughter. The donkey thought he would love to see the princess. He trotted up to the castle gate, took out his lute and began playing a marvellous tune.

The king and the court were in the great hall having dinner. When news arrived that a donkey sat outside the gate, playing the lute, the king ordered that the donkey be brought in to dine with them.

The king made sure that the donkey was served with the very best food and drink and was comfortable, and the donkey kept the king entertained with his talk.

After a while, when both the donkey and the king were really enjoying themselves, the lovely princess came into the great hall. She was so beautiful that the donkey was entranced, and could not take his eyes off her. The king noticed straight away and asked, "Little donkey, do you like my daughter?"

"Oh yes," he breathed, "I have never seen anyone as beautiful as she is."

"Then you will sit next to her too," said the king.

The donkey could not believe his luck as the king told his daughter to sit on the donkey's other side. The donkey served the princess with food and drink, and charmed her with conversation. He was kindness itself, and nothing was too much trouble.

By the end of the feast, the king liked the

donkey so much that he invited him to stay at the castle for as long as he wanted. By the end of one month, the king and the donkey had become firm friends. After six months, the king offered the donkey his daughter's hand in marriage. The donkey accepted joyfully, for he had fallen in love with her. The princess, however, was troubled. Although she had grown extremely fond of the donkey he was, after all, an animal. Who wanted a stable beast for a husband?

Still, a magnificent wedding was held. That night the donkey bolted the door of the bedchamber and checked that he and the princess were alone. Then he took off his donkey-skin and stood before the princess as a handsome prince. "This is who I am inside," he told her. "I have never been able to do this before, so no one has ever seen me like this."

The princess was overjoyed. She threw her arms around the prince and kissed him.

When morning came, the prince got up early and put his donkey-skin on again. Then he and the princess went to breakfast.

"How are you, my daughter?" whispered the old king, rather worried. "Are you sad?"

"Oh no, father," answered the princess. "I love my husband as much as if he were the most handsome man in the world."

The king was pleased, but astonished – and he guessed everything was not all as it seemed. That night he waited till the couple were asleep and then quietly opened the door to their bedchamber and peeked in. He was amazed to see a handsome prince lying in the bed and the donkey-skin flung on the ground. The king took the skin away and burnt it.

Early in the morning, the prince got up and went to put on his donkey-skin – but he could not find it anywhere. Then he began to panic. "Whatever will people say?" he cried in despair. "They won't believe it is me!"

But at that moment the king burst in, saying, "My son, do not worry. I know you are the donkey – you are loved whether you are in animal form or as this handsome prince. I will give you half my kingdom now and, when I die, you will rule over all of it."

The prince was delighted. He even went with the princess to visit his own family, who were thrilled to see him after all that time. And in time, the happy couple ruled together over not just one, but two kingdoms.

Jorinda and Joringel

There was once an old castle in the middle of a large, thick forest. In the castle lived an old woman who was a witch. She had the power to change herself into a cat or an owl. She could also lure wild creatures to her, so she could gobble them up. She had cast a spell around the castle so if anyone came within one hundred paces of it they were struck still like a statue. If a girl was trapped in this way, the witch would change her into a bird and keep her in a cage. She had about seven thousand cages of rare birds altogether!

In a nearby village, a beautiful girl called Jorinda had promised to marry a young man called Joringel. One summer's evening, they went for a walk through the forest. They were so involved in talking together that they did not pay attention to where they were going, and all of a sudden saw that they had strayed too near the witch's castle.

The moment they realized where they were, Jorinda disappeared and a nightingale stood in her place, singing sadly. Joringel was horrifed, but he could not move – he was frozen as though made of stone.

An owl swooped down from the sky and flapped into the undergrowth. A moment later, a crooked old woman walked out, with cruel eyes and a hooked nose that reached almost to her chin. She muttered to herself, caught the nightingale, and stumped off with it. Joringel could do nothing at all to stop her – he could not even cry out!

He stood helpless and, after some time, the old woman came back. All at once, Joringel found he was free and could move once more. He fell on his knees and begged the witch to give him back his beloved Jorinda. But she just laughed and said he would never see her again. Then she vanished!

Then Joringel wept as though his heart was breaking and ran around the forest calling Jorinda's name – but it was no use. In the end, he wandered away sadly.

Joringel thought about Jorinda every day, wondering how he was going to rescue her. Then one night he dreamt that he came across a blood-red flower growing in a meadow. He picked the flower and went to the witch's castle. Nothing could harm him, for the flower broke every evil spell!

When Joringel woke up, he went out searching for the blood-red flower. He looked high and low for eight days, and then on the ninth morning he found the flower growing in a meadow just like the one he had seen in his dream! Joringel picked it with trembling hands, then carried it carefully all the way back and into the witch's wood.

Closer and closer he came to her evil castle – when he was within one hundred paces of it, he found he was not struck still as he had been before, he could keep moving! Then he was full of joy and strode to the castle door. It was locked, but he touched it with the magic flower and it sprang open. Joringel rushed into the courtyard and listened for the sound of birds. There it was! He hurried in that direction and the birdsong grew louder and louder.

At last he came to a vast room filled with cages. The witch was there too, feeding all the birds! When she caught sight of Joringel, she jumped up and down in fury. "How did you get here?" she screeched. Claws sprang from her fingers and poison flew from her mouth. She rushed at him, but when she was just three paces away it was as if she hit an invisible wall – she beat her fists on the air and kicked and screamed, but she couldn't get any closer.

So Joringel drew up his courage and took no notice of her. He strode around the room, inspecting every cage. There were hundreds of nightingales! How would he know which one was his Jorinda?

As he stood there in despair, he noticed the witch quietly creeping towards the door – and she was carrying a cage with a nightingale in it.

Swiftly, he sprang towards the

old hag and touched her with the flower. At once, she was frozen like a statue, her powers gone. Next Joringel touched the nightingale with the flower – and Jorinda was standing there, throwing her arms around him, as beautiful as ever! Then they used the flower to turn all the other caged birds back into maidens so they could return home to their families.

The pair were married the very next week. The blood-red flower brought them luck in everything they did, and they lived the rest of their days in great happiness.